CW00858818
MMM

THIS Picture Knight BOOK
BELONGS TO

....

The Adventures of Maurice Mini Minor

GEOFFREY BAKER

Maurice visits old friends

illustrated by Rolf Harris

HODDER AND STOUGHTON

With thanks to the members of the Maidenhead Static Model Club for kind assistance

From an original idea by Dr P. Mansfield and Terry Moule

British Library Cataloguing in Publication Data

Baker, Geoffrey
Maurice visits old friends.
I. Title II. Harris, Rolf, *1930-* III. Series
823′.914 [J]

ISBN 0-340-52958-X

First published 1990 by Picture Knight

Published by Hodder and Stoughton Children's Books,
a division of Hodder and Stoughton Ltd,
Mill Road, Dunton Green, Sevenoaks, Kent TN13 2YA
Editorial office: 47 Bedford Square, London WC1E 7DP

Printed in Great Britain by Cambus Litho, East Kilbride

MMM
CH3 BTL
MIMI

'Whatever has happened?' yelled Maurice Mini Minor as he drove into the car park. Poor Bubbles was standing in a corner, very miserable and very downhearted, her whole body misted up with tears.

MMM

'Someone bumped into me,' she said mournfully. 'Someone just . . . well . . . bumped into me.'

'Someone bumped into her,' thundered Sir Reginald.

'An elephant or something,' said Cheeky Beetle.

'It couldn't have been a motor bike,' said Mr Splicer, and his wife agreed.

CH3BTL

Sure enough, Maurice could see that one of Bubble's headlights had been absolutely smashed and bent and buckled and, well, bumped.

'I know,' Maurice said, 'follow me. And slowly now; Bubbles has only one headlight remember.'

SPLICER

Off they went, out along the bypass and then down a little, leafy lane.

'This leads to the scrap yard,' cried Bubbles, slowing right down.

SCRAP
YARD

There ahead of them were hundreds and hundreds of old cars whose engines were too tired to work any more. Some were piled higgledy-piggledy on top of one another and others had been left on their own; grass and bright poppies growing up around them.

'It gives me the creeps,' blurted Bubbles, making them all jump.

'Here, here,' muttered Sir Reginald.

'We don't like it, do we?' said Mrs Splicer to her husband.

Cheeky Beetle giggled nervously.

SPLICER
CH3 BTL

'Goodness, gracious me,' cried Maurice, 'whatever is the matter with you all? Here are all our ancestors resting peacefully after years of driving all over the world and all you can do is complain. What strange idea has got into you?'

MMM

Nobody said a word and all was silent until a skylark flew up from the grass and sang as he soared into the sky.

Maurice drove round to face his friends. 'You should all be as happy as that skylark singing,' he said. 'These old cars have worked happily all their lives and soon they will be melted down and used again, as I hope I will be. It's just another beginning; nothing ever ends, you know.'

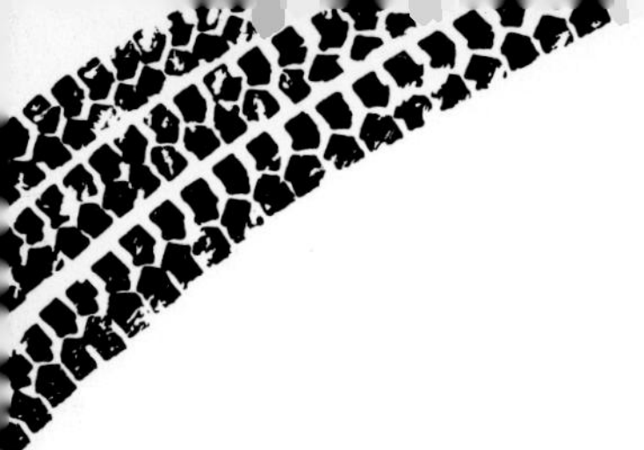

Sir Reginald, Mr and Mrs Splicer, Cheeky Beetle and poor Bubbles all listened carefully, without making a sound.

'What's more,' continued Maurice, 'some have left us good parts to use again and by golly gearsticks we will.'

'Here, here,' murmured Sir Reginald.

'Fine,' said Maurice. 'Now that's settled, how about us all looking for a new headlight for Bubbles?'

They all went off in different directions.

Suddenly, they heard Cheeky Beetle shouting, 'I've found one, I've found a headlight!'

MMM
SPLICE

'Where is it?' they cried excitedly.

'There,' said Cheeky Beetle.

They all looked *there* and, lying in the grass in front of them, was the most enormous headlight they had ever seen.

'That comes from a digger or a crane or something even bigger than that, silly,' said Maurice.

'It's a search-light,' said Sir Reginald, 'take my word for it, it's a search-light.'

'Yes,' said Cheeky Beetle, 'that's what we're doing, isn't it? Searching for a light!'

After they had finished laughing at Cheeky Beetle's joke – which didn't take very long – they began to search again.

CH3 BTL

Maurice and Bubbles drove round behind the big pile of cars. Maurice stared at one very old car with a folded down roof. 'I'm very grateful for being me,' Maurice said to himself accidentally aloud, 'but sometimes I dream of having thick leather seats and a roof that I could take off when it's sunny and a solid wooden dash-board and . . .'

Just then, they heard Mrs Splicer shouting, 'Here's one, here's one; right in front of us all the time!'

And so there was.

MMM
MMM

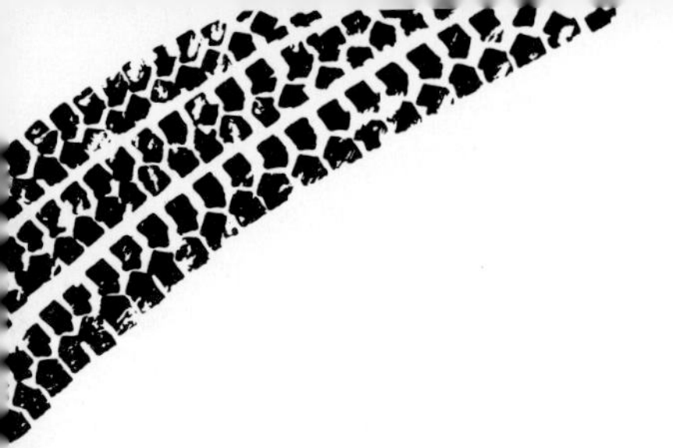

'It's wonderful,' yelled Bubbles, 'it's exactly the right one for me. All it needs is a polish and a little touch-up paint and I'll be able to see as well as ever.'

'Just think,' said Maurice, 'that headlight will be back on the road in no time, lighting up cat's-eyes for our dear friend, Bubbles. Perhaps one day, when we are resting here, we can help someone too. Let us be happy about that, not sad.'

'Hurrah for Maurice,' yelled Cheeky Beetle and everybody knew that he wasn't joking this time.

SPLICER

'Hurrah,' they all shouted and Maurice sang a song as he led them all back, through the town, to the car park.

Surrounded by the flowers
Serenaded by the lark,
We searched and found the perfect lamp,
To help us in the dark.

Listen everybody,
Who trembles at the sight,

Of dear old friends who've come to rest,
Remember Bubbles' light.

So
Don't be scared in the scrap yard,
Don't break down and cry,
If we take good care of the world we share,
The lark still sings in the sky.
Don't be scared in the scrap yard,
Nothing ever ends,
If we take good care of the world we share,
With all our faithful friends.

I sing this song as I drive along,
Maurice Mini Minor;
I get there soon 'cause I keep in tune,
Maurice Mini Minor;
And when you see me passing by,
Just toot your horn and wink your eye,
No need to wonder who am I,
Maurice Mini Minor.

MMM